THE MAN WHO CAME BACK

Graphic Novel

Catherine J Elliss

This is a work of fiction. All of the characters, names, incidents, organizations, and dialogue in this novel are either the products of the author's imagination or are used fictitiously.

WestBow Press books may be ordered through booksellers or by contacting:

WestBow Press
A Division of Thomas Nelson & Zondervan
1663 Liberty Drive
Bloomington, IN 47403
www.westbowpress.com
1 (866) 928-1240

Because of the dynamic nature of the Internet, any web addresses or links contained in this book may have changed since publication and may no longer be valid. The views expressed in this work are solely those of the author and do not necessarily reflect the views of the publisher, and the publisher hereby disclaims any responsibility for them.

Any people depicted in stock imagery provided by Getty Images are models, and such images are being used for illustrative purposes only. Certain stock imagery © Getty Images.

Illustrations by Ngariki Teariki.
Author photo photographed by Louann Teariki

Scripture taken from the New King James Version®. Copyright © 1982 by Thomas Nelson. Used by permission. All rights reserved.

ISBN: 978-1-9736-8882-2 (sc)
ISBN: 978-1-9736-8883-9 (e)

Library of Congress Control Number: 2020905178

Print information available on the last page.

WestBow Press rev. date: 3/27/2020

WestBow
PRESS®
A DIVISION OF THOMAS NELSON
& ZONDERVAN

Once upon a time, in a far, far northern village in China, there lived a little boy. He lived on a farm with his mum and his sister. They had so much fun every day. Their lives were filled with love. They only to step out the door and there was more love. In fact, on the same farm in another house, there lived the boy's grandparents.

The little boy, Afu Ling, with his sister and mother lived untouched by the world, or so it seemed to the little boy. They would play near the fireplace inside or outside in the snow.

On the way to school, the little boy would pop in to see his grandparents next door. They were much like the older people from Charlie and the Chocolate Factory, also known as Willy Wonka & the Chocolate Factory. Just like Charlie's uncles and aunties, Afu Ling's grandparents loved to spoil him. They gave him chocolate and soft drink before school. It was no wonder that as a little boy Afu Ling looked more like an oompa loompa with a thick parka on! Poor Afu Ling's mother would just shake her head and wonder, "What could she do?" as she rushed out the door to take the kids to school before she ran to work. There was no dad in sight.

As the boy grew, he came to love exercise and using his body. In particular, he loved to chop wood. Everyone loved this little boy who always made sure others were enjoying themselves. He was fun to be around.

As a young man, Afu Ling decided to venture off to the big city, Beijing. Tales were heard back in his village of his great success. Tales of him traveling all over the world, of skiing, bungee jumping and sailing in New Zealand, and mountain biking in Peru. By now, he had taken on a Western nickname, Tom, named after his favorite action star, Tom Cruise, of *Mission Impossible* fame.

Later still the young man travelled further and went to live in the sun, in the exotic far away land of Hawaii where the local people were known all over the world for their friendly smiles and warm hospitality.

The young man was even more popular. The village heard of, and saw online, his new achievements and new titles. He went to America and saw the Statue of Liberty and even the Taj Mahal in India.

Then one day the little boy, now a man, came back. He didn't want to meet any of his old friends. But back on the farm in the house he grew up in, new times of love, laughter and winter warmth were had. Afu Ling (or Tom), with his sister, their beloved mum and now his niece and nephew, laughed and played. In winter, they played video games and sometimes out in the snow.

In spring, they jumped on the trampoline
and flew kites up on the mountain.

The village heard he was back and wondered... 'Why he wasn't married? Where was his money? Why wasn't he working?' On the farm all was unchanged, or at least it seemed to Afu Ling, and that life outside the farm didn't matter.

One day an old man came to the farm to buy his firewood. He saw Afu Ling and remembered his smile and laugh. He was reminded of the young boy so many years before. He also wondered the same things as the town's people nearby.

Another time the old man came to buy his firewood, he saw Afu Ling outside doing Kung Fu. He couldn't help but smile. It seemed Afu Ling was trying to teach himself.

The old man was a Kung Fu master and many years before he had taught Kung Fu. For some reason he felt drawn to this younger man, perhaps as he remembered he did not have a father. So he calmly walked over and joined in the slow warm up exercises that he had once known so well.

Afu Ling acknowledged the old man with a smile. Words were not needed, the old man began to teach the younger man. He began to come two or three times a week. Often, he would share wisdom. He knew the younger man did not like to be instructed on how to think so he was careful to not say much but give some simple sayings every now and then.

"There is a way that seems right to a man, but its end is the way of death." Proverbs 14:12

And

"All the ways of a man are pure in his own eyes, but the LORD weighs the spirits." Proverbs 16:2

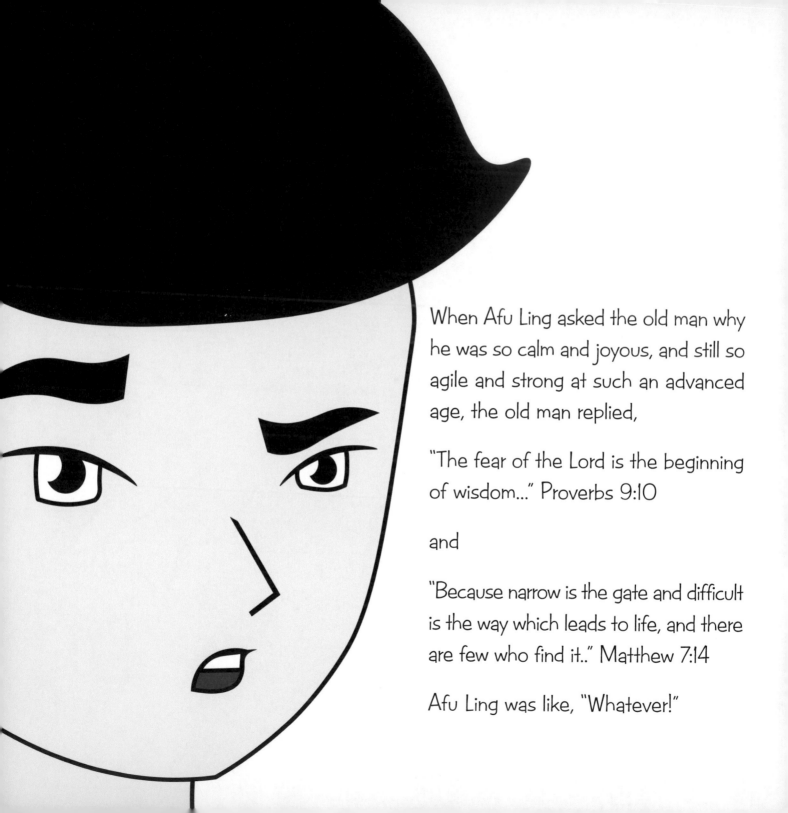

When Afu Ling asked the old man why he was so calm and joyous, and still so agile and strong at such an advanced age, the old man replied,

"The fear of the Lord is the beginning of wisdom..." Proverbs 9:10

and

"Because narrow is the gate and difficult is the way which leads to life, and there are few who find it.." Matthew 7:14

Afu Ling was like, "Whatever!"

The old man continued to come two or three times per week all through spring and into summer. Afu Ling was becoming stronger and more disciplined. Finally, the old man asked, "Why aren't you working?" Afu Ling replied, "My goal is just to be. Have a good time. Be happy. All is good. " The old man continued on with the Kung Fu briefly, then just shook his head and walked away until another day.

Over time, the old man knew he needed to step up and mentor this young man who must have lacked male discipline and mentoring in his life. "A man's role in life is to be the provider, and spiritual head of his family." The younger man laughed, "I do not have my own family. I have the best mother and sister in the world." As the old man undertook the Kung Fu training that day he pushed the younger man harder and harder, until he was physically exhausted.

Another time, the young man probed the old man about his own family. The old man said how his children had families of their own and lived far away in Nanjing. His wife was at home wondering what he was doing out there with the younger man. She was his sweetheart. He had been a slow starter in life and had been stubborn and rebellious, just as this younger man was. Perhaps that was why he was so patient with him. He could see this younger man had promise, but then so did many others and yet many live a life of discontent. He was also becoming angry at this younger man, could he not see that life was for living? Life is not a dress rehearsal. His own motto was to make each day count as if it is your last.

The old man shared more wisdom, this time about love. "A real man provides for his family, protects them and professes that they are his." The young man smiled, laughed and said, "Whatever!" The old man just shook his head and left, this time without finishing the routine but instead gave a long leap at a small tree and snapped it clean off.

SNAP!

The young man was surprised. He thought all was good in his life. He got on well with the old man and shouldn't the old man be happy that someone of his younger age was happy to be around him?

huh ?

The old man did not come around that week or the next.

Then one night there was a black out. Afu Ling's mum was out and there were no distractions like the television, the internet or video games. He remembered he had loved a beautiful woman once. Initially he had taken her out and paid for everything, even protected her from wild dogs and dangerous people, and he had professed his love for her to her many times over the years they were together on and off. His work and his heart had kept him moving.

Some only knew her as his wife, others never knew she had ever existed. He remembered them laughing and loving, traveling and living in different places in the sun and in the rain of the tropical wet season and in the winter in Utah. He had even told her on numerous occasions that she was his family. He had promised her and her parents that he would protect her and provide for her. But he hadn't kept that promise, any of the times he promised it.

Meanwhile the old man was wondering why he was even bothering with the younger man. Afu Ling, as a young boy seemed to have been struggling to be a man from such a young age, perhaps to be the man of the house for his mother. And yet as an adult of many years, here he was seemingly struggling to be that little boy again. Who must have only felt loved when everyone else was sacrificing everything for him. The old man's wife supported her husband faithfully and occasionally added in her own comments. The wife was not as patient as the old man. She just snorted, "He is just selfish and lazy, expecting everyone else to pay for his own life. Can't you make him go out and get a job? Even if he chooses to never have his own family, he can at least be earning his own money and paying his own way. What example is that setting to those around him?" The old man just shook his head and walked away.

The old man returned to the farm one day and the younger man wasn't there. His mother was. She was crying tears of joy. She explained that she had finally heard the words from her cherished son that she now realised she had been waiting many years to hear.

Afu Ling had told her, "I know now what I need to do. I need to face my greatest fear of becoming the man I know I am destined to be. It is time for me to grow up and take responsibility for my own life."

The End

Printed in the United States
By Bookmasters